D0871231

HECTOR AND THE NOISY NEIGHBOR

David Gavril

Dial Books for Young Readers *New York*

Published by Dial Books for Young Readers
A division of Penguin Young Readers Group
345 Hudson Street
New York, New York 10014

Designed by Nancy R. Leo-Kelly
Text set in Berkeley
Manufactured in China on acid-free paper
1 3 5 7 9 10 8 6 4 2

Library of Congress Cataloging-in-Publication Data
Gavril, David.
Hector and the noisy neighbor / by David Gavril.
p.   cm.
Summary: After Hector the rabbit finally tells his new neighbor
Rutherford the pig that he is too noisy, they become friends.
ISBN 0-8037-2808-5
[1. Noise—Fiction. 2. Neighbors—Fiction.
3. Interpersonal relations—Fiction.
4. Musical groups—Fiction. 5. Rabbits—Fiction.
6. Pigs—Fiction.] I. Title.
PZ7.G2358 He 2004   [E]—dc21   2002004706

The artwork was created with pencil, ink, and watercolor.

For my parents

One afternoon Hector noticed that the vacant apartment in his building had been rented.

"Oh dear," thought Hector. "I have a new neighbor. Things have been so nice and peaceful since Sammy Snorzsalot moved out."

Hector began to worry. What if the new neighbor was loud? Hector's paws felt sweaty. His whiskers began to twitch. "I'd better go talk to the landlord and see what I can find out."

But the landlord was in his room hibernating.

Hector opened a book and waited.

Soon a station wagon pulled up. The driver got out and banged on Hector's window.

"Hello!" he yelled. "I am Rutherford, your new neighbor." And with a happy snort, he began unloading his car.

"Oh, no," thought Hector. "Another loud one."

That afternoon as Hector lay down for his nap, he was star-
tled by a loud noise. *"BBBBbBbBRRRRattt!"* Rutherford had
just unpacked his trombone.

All week Hector heard noises coming from the other side of the wall. The door slammed as Rutherford went in and out. His hoofs clomped heavily as he moved about. And it seemed that every night he was moving furniture and hanging pictures.

Hector felt like screaming.

"Perhaps he doesn't realize how much noise he's making. But how can I tell him without offending him?" He decided to consult his advice book.

In the chapter "Pig Problems," he read: "The way to win over a pig is through his stomach."

"I know," Hector thought. "I'll bake some mud pies and leave a note telling him my problem."

When the pies were done, Hector wrote on a napkin and rang Rutherford's doorbell.

"Thank you," said Rutherford. "These will make a wonderful dessert."

Back at home, Hector settled into a nice bubble bath. But it wasn't long before the noise started up again.

"Didn't Rutherford see my note?" Hector wondered.

His ears stood up on his head. "Oh dear," he thought. "What am I to do?" His nose quivered nervously. "I know! I'll invite him over for dinner and speak to him then."

Hector was setting the table when Rutherford arrived.

"That smells scrumptious," Rutherford remarked. "I'll have seconds!"

Hector served Rutherford two bowls of stew and took a carrot for himself. Rutherford grinned and smacked his lips.

"He seems to be enjoying himself," Hector thought. "Perhaps now is a good time to tell him."

"There's nothing as relaxing as a QUIET evening at home," Hector hinted.

"Slurp," said Rutherford.

"And QUIET neighbors do make the best of friends. Wouldn't you agree?"

"Your cooking does agree with me," Rutherford replied between bites.

Hector blushed happily. "This is going very well," he thought.

When Rutherford had gone and the dishes were washed, Hector sat down in his favorite chair. Soon his whole room was vibrating. THUMP! SLAP! PING!

"More noise!" Hector groaned. "I'd hoped I was getting through to him."

Exasperated, Hector threw his book across the room. It made a satisfying thud against the wall. "Hmm," he thought. "Perhaps if Rutherford hears noise from me, he'll realize how much I can hear from him."

Hector put on his heavy winter boots and stomped around in circles.

Then he got out his ladder and practiced jumping down from the top rung.

After that, he set up a drum kit and began wailing away. BOOM! BANG! CLANG! He was having so much fun that he almost didn't hear the doorbell.

"What's the matter, Rutherford?" cried Hector. "Can't you take a little noise?"

"What noise?" said Rutherford. "I came over to tell you that you're a real ace with those sticks."

But Hector wasn't listening. "Noise! Noise! Noise!" he said. "That's all I've heard since you moved in!" And he stomped back to his drums and banged even harder.

"Was I being loud?" asked Rutherford. "I'm sorry. Why didn't you say something?"

"I tried," said Hector. "But I didn't want to hurt your feelings."

Rutherford nodded. "I'll try to be less noisy," he said.

Hector and Rutherford were quiet for a moment.

"You know," Hector said, eyeing his drum set, "I was really enjoying playing the drums. Would you like to play with me?"

"Yippee!" said Rutherford. "I'll go get my horn."

Hector pounded out a thunderous beat, and Rutherford blasted a few notes on his trombone. The floor shook and the windows rattled.

Suddenly, a deep baritone bellowed from the stairway. It was Borislav, the landlord. "Be quiet up there!" he growled. "Some of us are trying to hibernate!"

"Pardon me," said Rutherford. "But would you growl again?"

"*GGGGRRRHHH!*" said Borislav.

"And a little louder?"

"*GGGGRRRRRRHHHH!*" Borislav rumbled.

"What pipes!" said Rutherford. "You have a gorgeous growl. Would you like to join our band?"

"*Hot diggety!*" Borislav roared. "I've always wanted to be a singer."

From that day on, Rutherford did his noisy things in the
morning while Hector was out at the library.

In the evening Hector read his books while Rutherford
worked out at the gym. And more often than not, the building
was peaceful and quiet.

But every afternoon at four o'clock, the group met in the laundry room and raised the roof!